Where's My Mommy?

Where's My Mommy?

By K. T. Hao • Illustrated by Alessandra Toni

Purple Bear Books • New York

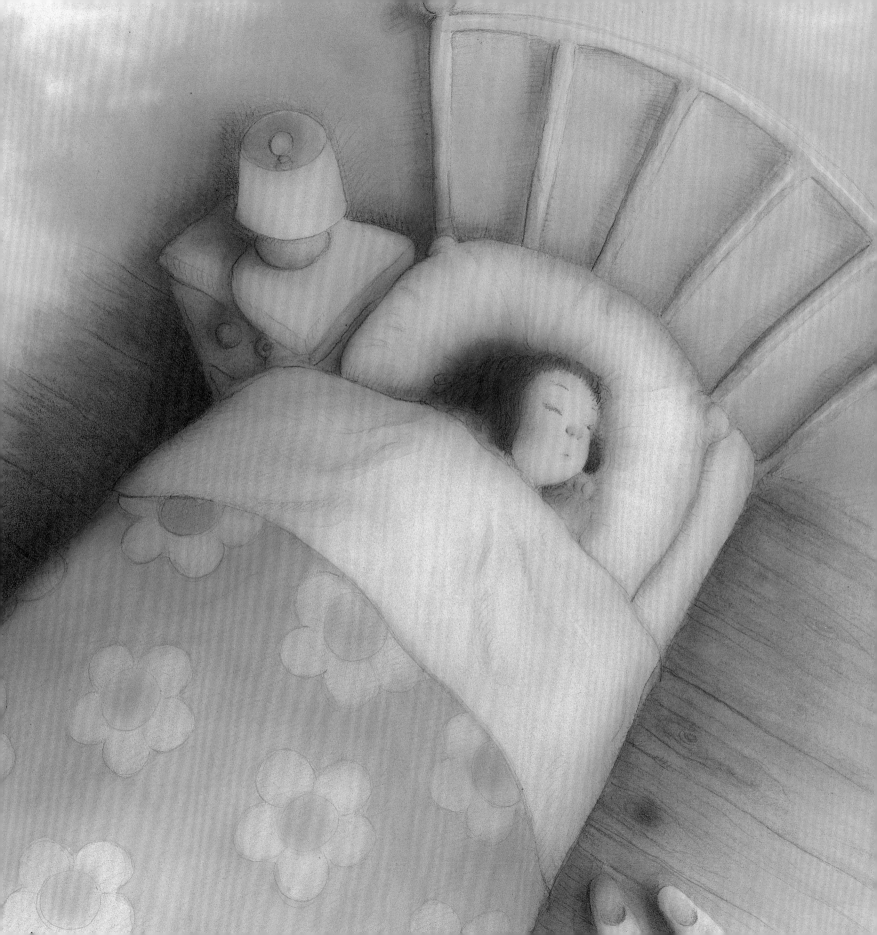

One cool autumn night, Polly snuggled into bed, waiting for her mommy to give her a good-night kiss. She had just drifted off to sleep, when suddenly she was awakened by a strange noise.

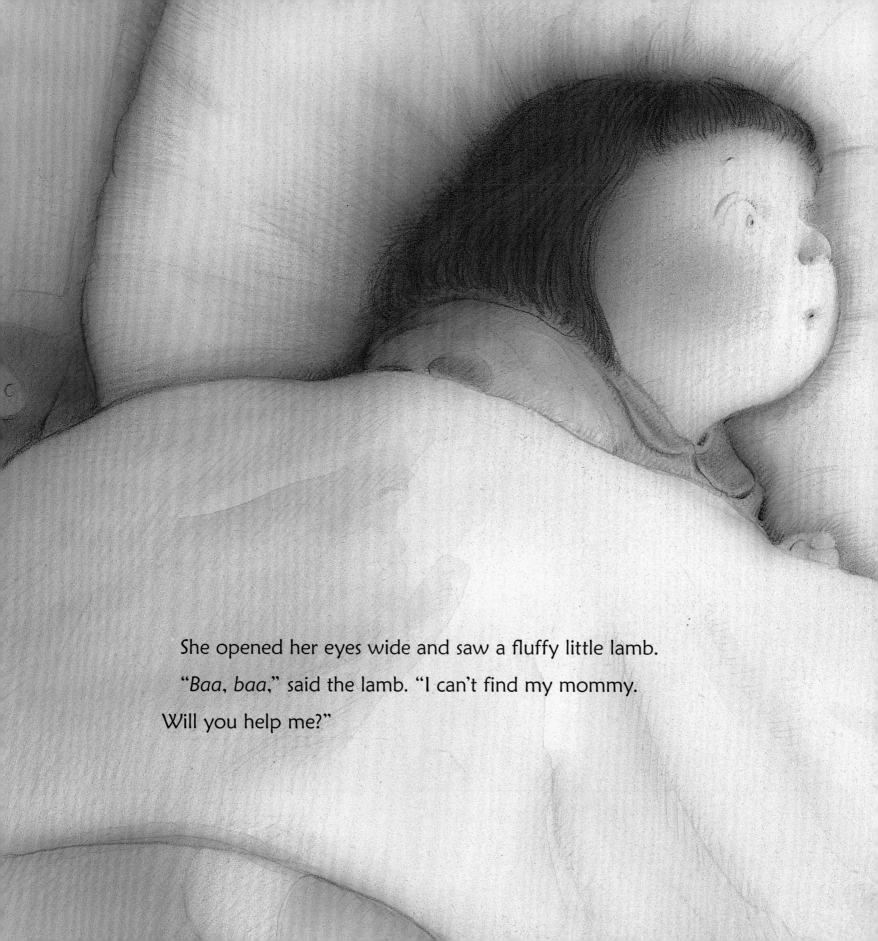

She opened her eyes wide and saw a fluffy little lamb.

"*Baa, baa*," said the lamb. "I can't find my mommy.

Will you help me?"

"Of course I will. Come on, let's go see if we can find her."

As they went outside the little lamb spotted something in the distance.

"Look!" he cried. "Is that my mommy?"

Polly laughed. "This isn't your mommy. This is a rabbit."

"You're right," said the lamb. "My mommy has four legs like this rabbit, but she's much taller. . . . Wait! Is that her?"

The lamb scampered away and Polly ran after him.

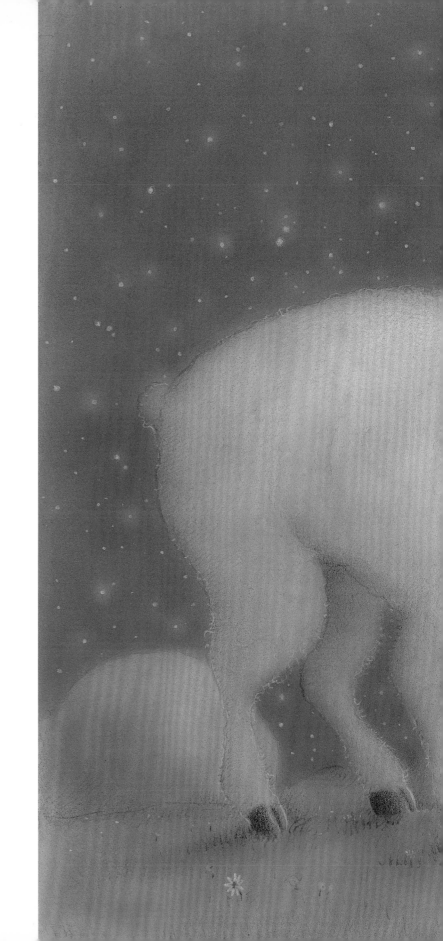

"This isn't my mommy," said the lamb.

"Nope," said Polly. "This is a giraffe. She has four legs and she's taller than a rabbit, but if your mommy was this tall you wouldn't be able to reach her sweet milk. Come on, let's keep looking."

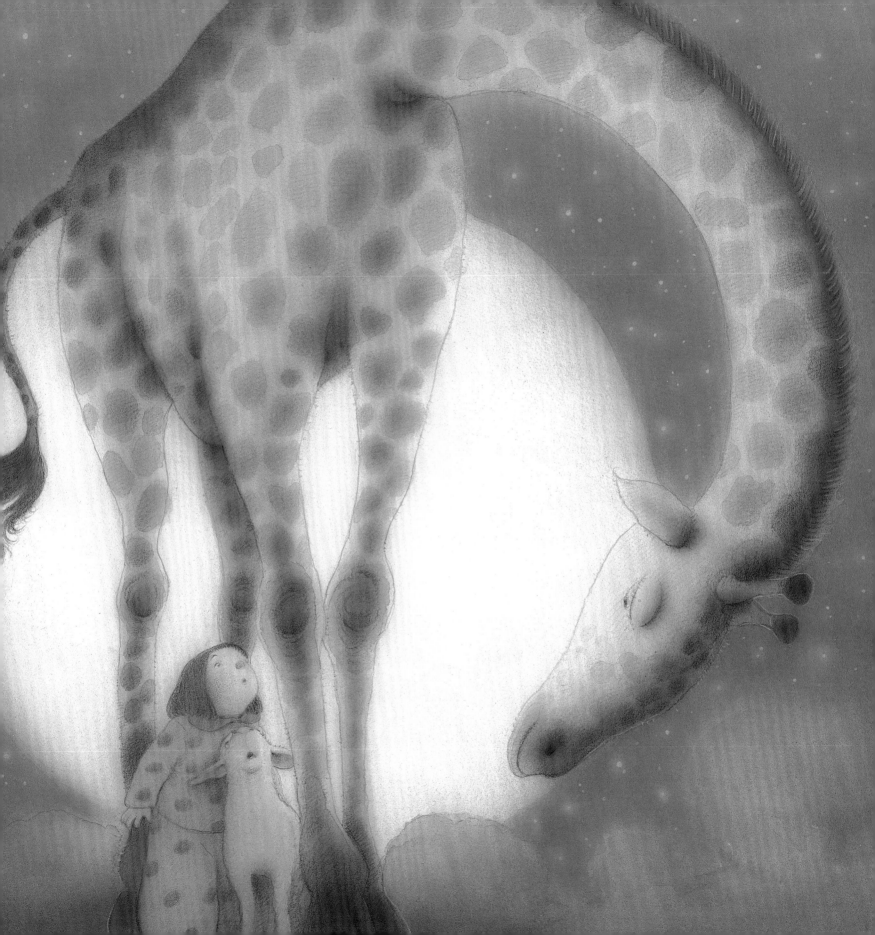

"Who's *that*?" asked the little lamb. "She has four legs, she's not too tall, and she looks like she has milk—but she's not my mommy."

"It's a cow," said Polly. "Your mommy has a soft white coat like yours."

The lamb looked around and shouted, "There she is!"

But as they got closer, the little lamb hung his head and said sadly, "She is not my mommy."

"No," said Polly. "She's a polar bear. She does have a soft white coat, but your mommy doesn't eat fish, she eats grass."

Polly and the little lamb kept walking until they came to a big meadow.

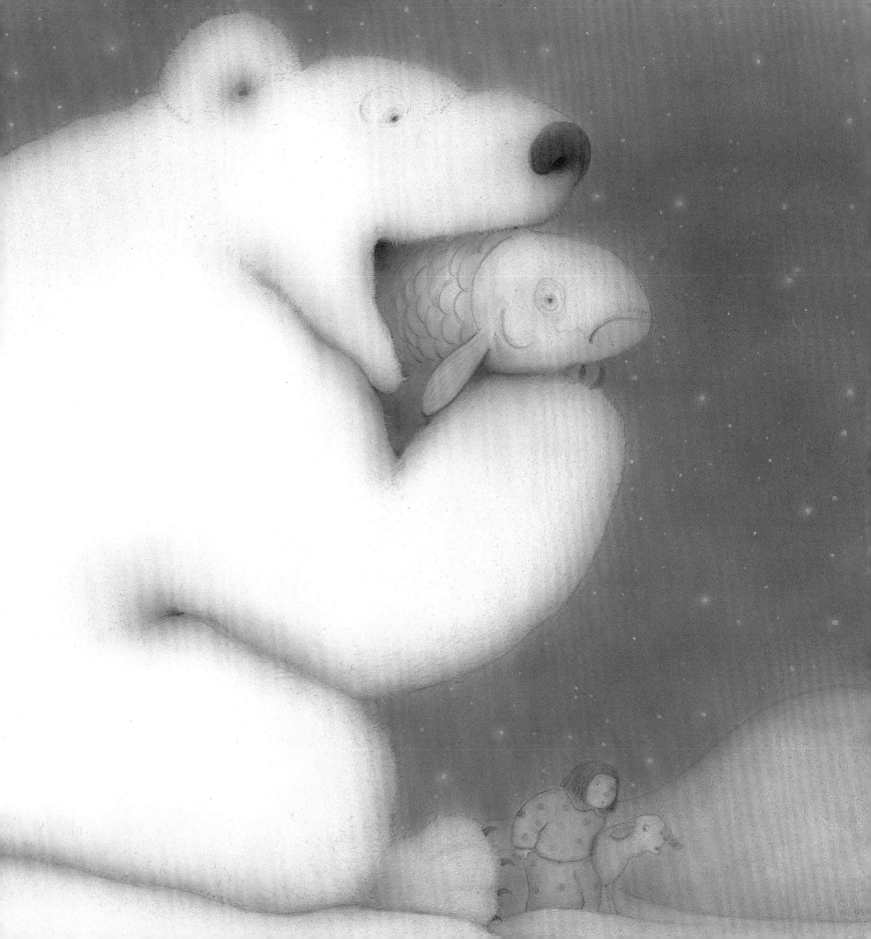

"Look at her" whispered the lamb. "She has four legs, she's not too tall, she's all white, and she's eating grass—but she's not my mommy either."

"I'm sorry," Polly whispered. "That's a beautiful white horse. When she calls her baby she says, *neigh, neigh.* Your mommy would say *baa, baa.*"

Polly and the little lamb kept
on walking until they saw a herd
of animals in the distance.

"They have four legs," said Polly.

"And they're not too tall," said
the little lamb.

"And they're eating grass," said Polly.

"And they have soft white coats, just like mine!" said the little lamb excitedly, as one of them turned around.

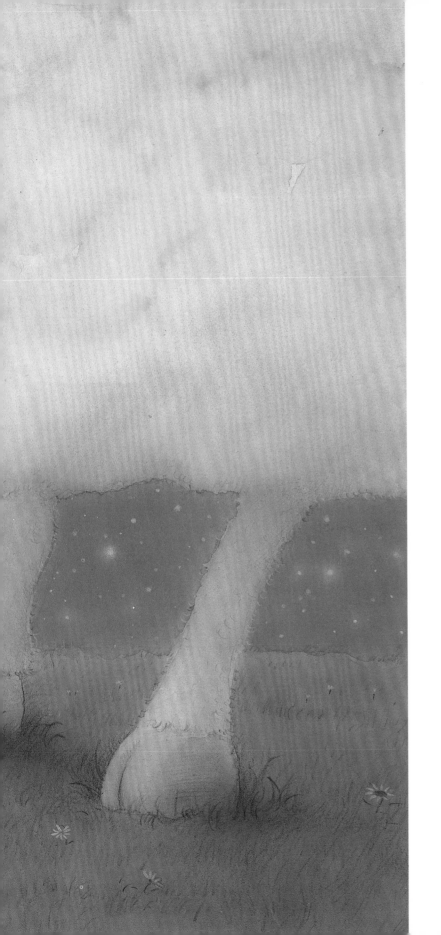

"Mommy!" shouted the little lamb as he bounded across the field.

"My baby!" exclaimed the little lamb's mommy. "I've been looking *everywhere* for you!"

Polly waved good-bye and hurried home. She hadn't realized it was so late.

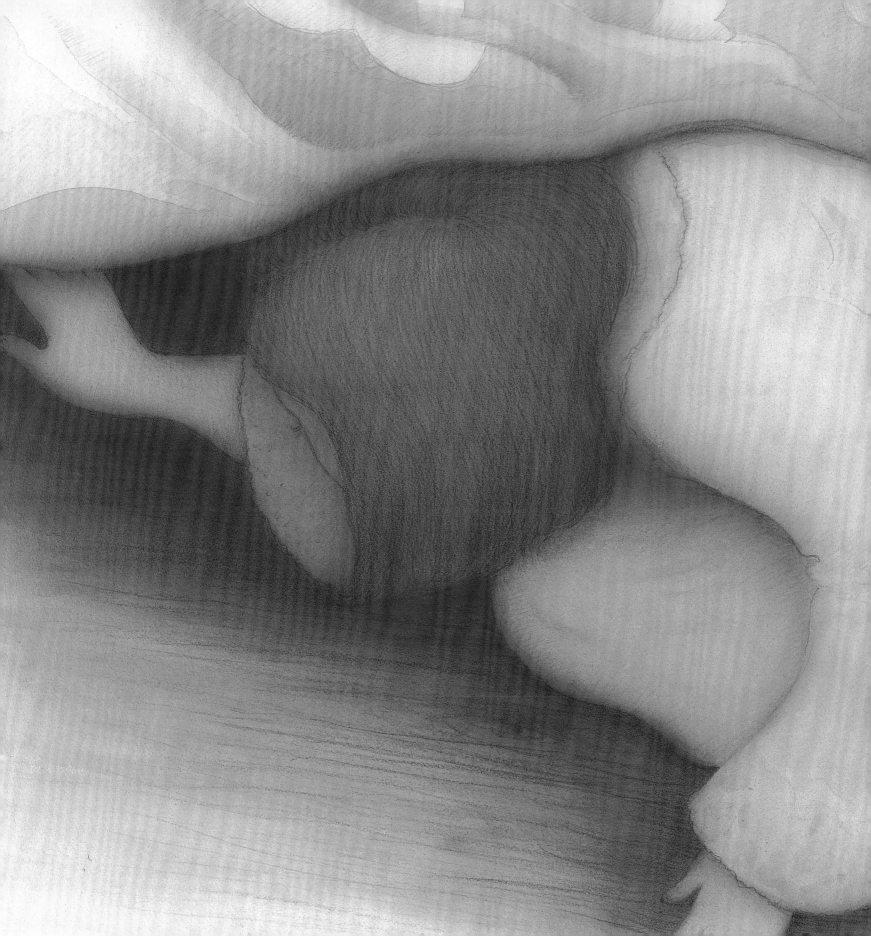

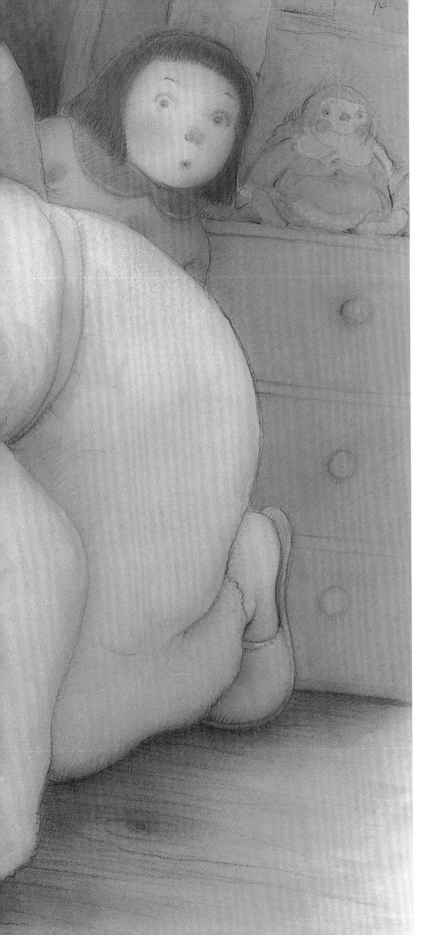

"Mommy?" she said quietly.

"My baby!" exclaimed her mother,
as she hugged Polly tightly. "I've been
looking *everywhere* for you!"

Polly snuggled into bed and told her mommy how she had helped the little lamb.

"Mommy," she asked, "if I got lost, would you come and find me?"

"Of course I would! I would find you if you were a little lost lamb, a bunny rabbit, a baby giraffe, cow, or horse—even a polar bear cub."

"Good night, Mommy. I love you."

"Good night, baby. I love you too."

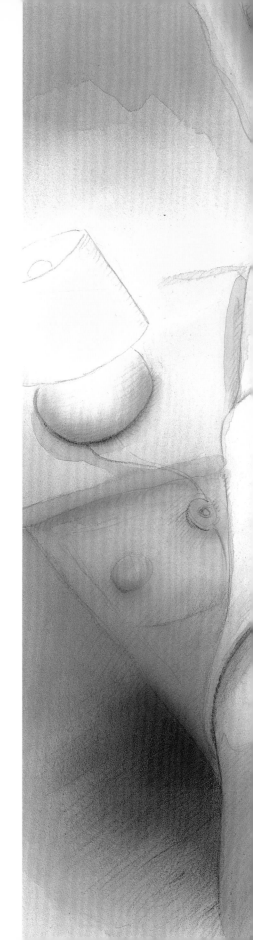

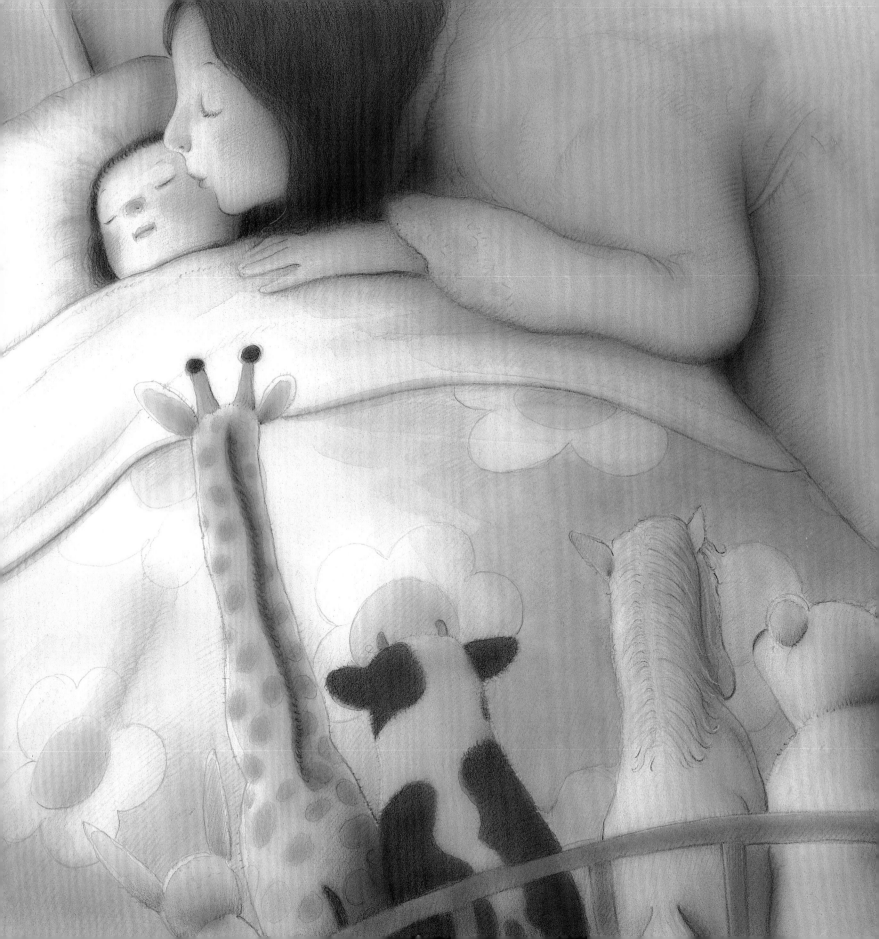

TRANSLATED BY ANNIE KUNG

Text copyright © 2007 by K. T. Hao

Illustrations copyright © 2007 by Alessandra Toni

English translation copyright © 2008 by Purple Bear Books Inc., New York

First published in Taiwan by Grimm Press

First English-language edition published in 2008 by Purple Bear Books Inc., New York

For more information about our books, visit our website: purplebearbooks.com

Library of Congress Cataloging-in-Publication Data is available.

This edition prepared by Cheshire Studio.

Printed in Taiwan

Trade edition

ISBN-10: 1-933327-40-5

ISBN-13: 978-1-933327-40-2

1 3 5 7 9 TE 10 8 6 4 2

Library edition

ISBN-10: 1-933327-41-3

ISBN-13: 978-1-933327-41-9

1 3 5 7 9 LE 10 8 6 4 2